Usborne

Five-Minute Bedtime Stories

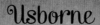

Usborne

Five-Minute
Bedtime
Stories

Sam Taplin

Illustrated by Ag Jatkowska

Designed by Kasia Dudziuk

Cover design by Nancy Leschnikoff

Contents

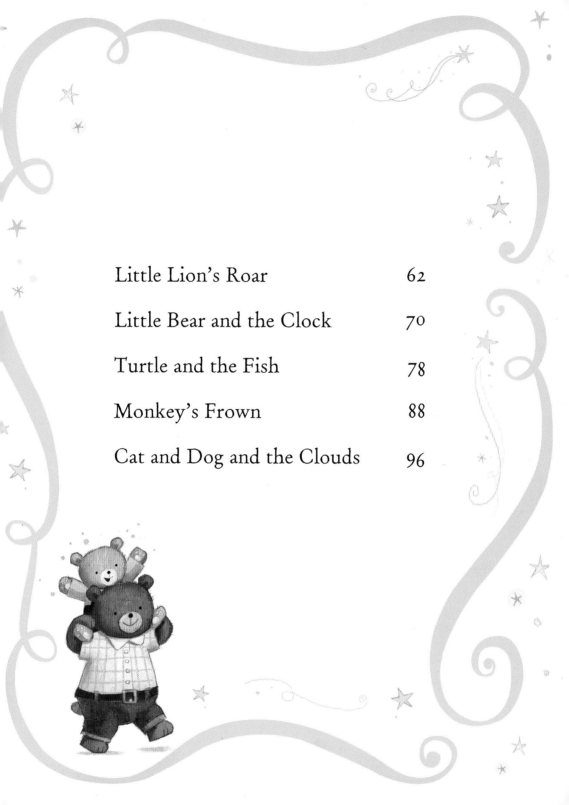

Dog
and the
Balloon

One afternoon, Dog was walking home from the fairground with a big red balloon, and he was feeling happy. He liked the sunshine and he liked the breeze and he liked his balloon that blew around above the treetops. Life was perfect... except for one thing.

"I wish I had someone to play with," said Dog to himself. "That would be nice."

Dog stopped and looked
around – left and right and up
and down – but there was no
one else there. So he walked on.

Just before he reached the path to
his cottage, he spotted something yellow
in the sky, popping up over the hill.

"It's another balloon," thought Dog.
"I wonder who's holding it?"

"HELLO?" he shouted. "WHO ARE YOU?"
But it was a long way to the other side of the hill,
and he didn't hear anyone answer.

"Maybe they can see my balloon too," he thought.
So he waved it from side to side, to see if anything
would happen. But nothing did. Dog sighed.
"Oh well," he said, "never mind."

But then he noticed that the yellow balloon had started moving. It was bobbing from side to side, just like his had been. He stared at it. "Is it just blowing around in the wind?" he thought. "No, I think it's waving at me!"

This made Dog very excited, and he started jumping around, making his balloon go up and down. After a few seconds, he saw the yellow balloon bob up and down as well.

"YES!" he shouted. "I CAN SEE YOU!" But he still didn't hear any reply. He stood there for a while and wondered what to do. Then he had an idea.

"WAIT THERE!" he shouted. And he ran back to his cottage.

When he got home, he found a piece of writing paper and sat down with his pen. And this is what he wrote:

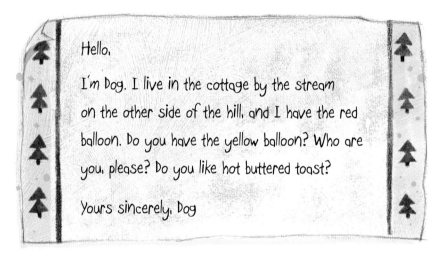

Hello,

I'm Dog. I live in the cottage by the stream on the other side of the hill, and I have the red balloon. Do you have the yellow balloon? Who are you, please? Do you like hot buttered toast?

Yours sincerely, Dog

"That will do," said Dog. He tied his letter to the balloon and went out again. This time there was no sign of the yellow balloon. He threw his red balloon into the sky, then watched it float further and further away until it disappeared over the hill.

He stood there for a while, wondering if the yellow balloon might come back. But it didn't.

Dog was quite tired after all the balloon-flying and letter-writing, so he went back to his cottage for some hot buttered toast and a nap.

After a while he woke up, but he wasn't sure why. "I was having such a nice dream," he thought. "Something must have made a noise." He looked around his room but he couldn't see anything noisy, so he slowly drifted back to sleep.

"Ah yes," he murmured, "I was dreaming about eating buttered toast with a friend… this was a lovely dream."

But all of a sudden he woke up again. He opened one eye and stared around the room, but it all looked normal and he couldn't hear anything. Everything was quiet for a while, and then…

KNOCK, KNOCK, KNOCK…

"Oh," thought Dog, "someone's at the door."
He hurried over and opened it and he found...
...a big yellow balloon sitting on his doorstep.
"Um, hello?" said Dog.

"Hello," said the balloon. "Is this the cottage
by the stream please?"

"I... er, yes, it is," said Dog. "So you got
my letter then?"

"Yes," said the balloon, "and I do like
buttered toast. It's what I like best."

"I've... er... I've never met a balloon that liked buttered toast before," said Dog.

The balloon shifted around and wobbled, and ever so slowly a little face with ears and whiskers popped up from behind it.

"No," said the face, "it's me who likes it."

And that's the story of how Cat and Dog became friends.

Little Tiger
and the
Island

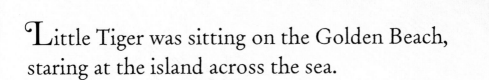

Little Tiger was sitting on the Golden Beach, staring at the island across the sea.

"I wish I could swim," he thought. "Then I could go to the island – it looks lovely over there." He gazed at the palm trees and the mountains on the island and stretched one of his paws towards the water, but he didn't put it in.

Just then there was a splash, and Little Tiger's friend Turtle popped up out of the sea.

"Hello!" said Turtle. "I've been to the island. All the flowers are out, and the dolphins are singing."

"Oh," said Little Tiger. "I wish I could go."

"Of course you can go," said Turtle. "Let's swim across now and have lunch in the secret lagoon."

Little Tiger looked up at the great big sea, then down at his small paws.

"I don't think so, Turtle," he said. "I think I'm a tiger who can't swim."

"OK," said Turtle, "we won't swim. But let's just have a dip in the water. That can't hurt, can it?"

Little Tiger looked at Turtle. "You're not trying to trick me, are you?" he said.
"No, no," said Turtle, "we won't swim."

So Little Tiger stepped slowly into the water.

"Now," said Turtle, "I'll tell you what's fun –
waving your feet up and down, like this."
So Little Tiger tried it.

"Yes I quite like waving my paws," he said.
"If only swimming was this simple..."

"Never mind," said Turtle, "let's keep doing it."

So Little Tiger kept
waving his paws...

...and as he waved them, he noticed something.

"The island seems to be coming closer!" he said.

"Oh yes," said Turtle. "It's probably swimming. The island likes to swim sometimes. Just keep waving your feet." So Little Tiger did.

And the island came closer...

...and closer...

...and closer, until all of a sudden Little Tiger could feel the warm sand under his paws.

"How incredible," he said. "I'm so happy the island decided to swim. Now you can show me the secret lagoon, and we can go and play with the dolphins."

Turtle gave Little Tiger a smile. "Islands can't swim," he said. "Look behind you."

When Little Tiger turned around,
he stopped and stared. The great blue
sea was stretching out behind him.

Far away in the distance he could see
the Golden Beach where he and Turtle
had been sitting just a little while ago.

"I... I... don't understand," he said.

"We swam to the island," smiled Turtle.
"You're a good little swimmer."

For a moment Little Tiger didn't know what to
say, then he thought about being cross with Turtle
for tricking him, but he was so glad about being
able to swim that he decided to be happy after all.

"I can swim!" he shouted, and he went for another
little dip to celebrate.

"I told you you could do it,"
laughed Turtle. "Now come and
meet the eagles and the elephants."
So they ran off into the palm trees and spent
all day having adventures on the island.

When the evening came and the sun was setting,
Little Tiger was tired. "I think I'm a bit too sleepy
for more swimming," he said.

"That's OK," said Turtle. "Just curl up on my
back." And Little Tiger fell fast asleep as Turtle
carried him all the way home.

Squirrel's Holiday

One snowy afternoon, Squirrel was sitting at home knitting a scarf and waiting for something interesting to happen. And then, to her surprise, it did – something popped through her letterbox. So she hurried over to see what it might be...

It was a letter. And this is what it said:

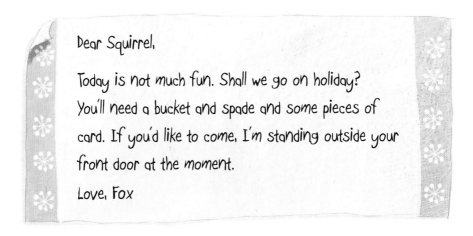

> Dear Squirrel,
>
> Today is not much fun. Shall we go on holiday?
> You'll need a bucket and spade and some pieces of
> card. If you'd like to come, I'm standing outside your
> front door at the moment.
> Love, Fox

Squirrel opened the door, and there was Fox
carrying some deck chairs and a camera.

"Hello," said Squirrel. "Yes, I'd love to come on
holiday!" So she fetched her things and they set off.

"I've never been on holiday before," said Squirrel.
"Where are we going?"

"Oh," said Fox, "I hadn't thought about that."

They looked around them at the snowy woods.

"How does it work?" said Squirrel. "Why are we bringing chairs and a bucket and spade?"

"I'm not sure," said Fox. "That's what everyone takes on holiday. I expect we'll work it out."
They walked a bit further and stopped by a tree.

"Let's start here," said Fox, "and see how it goes."
"OK," said Squirrel. "What do we do?"

"I think we sit in these chairs," said Fox.

So they sat in their chairs for a while and waited to see what would happen.

"Has the holiday started yet?" asked Squirrel.

"I don't know," said Fox. "It's hard to tell, isn't it?"

"Are we supposed to do something with the bucket and spade?" said Squirrel.

"I think we build castles," said Fox. "Shall we try?"

So they took their spade and filled the bucket right to the top with snow, then tipped it out to make a castle. They made a few more, then they had a rest.

"I think maybe we're on holiday now,"
said Fox. "This feels quite holiday-ish to me."

"What about the cards I brought?"
said Squirrel. "What do we do with those?"

"I think we write about what a nice time we're
having on holiday," said Fox, "and then we send
them to our friends."

"That sounds fun," said Squirrel. "I'll write mine."

Dear Fox, I'm on holiday with you at the moment, and I'm
having a very nice time. Hope you are too. Love, Squirrel

"Thank you," said Fox. "And here's one for you."

Dear Squirrel, I'm having a very nice time on holiday.
And so are you, because you've just told me. Love, Fox

Then a bear came walking past. "What are you two
doing sitting here in the snow?" he said.

"We think we're on holiday," said Squirrel.
"But we're not sure. Would you mind taking
a picture, so we can remember our day?"

So the bear took a picture of them while they
stood by their snow castles and smiled.

"Thank you," said Squirrel. "By the way, do you
know what a holiday is?"

"Hmm," said the bear, "I think it means when you go away from home and have a really nice time."

"In that case," said Squirrel, "we're on holiday!"

"Shall we go home now?" said Fox.

"OK," said Squirrel. "But I think we should go on holiday again tomorrow."

"What a good idea," said Fox.

And they did.

Little Rabbit
and the
World

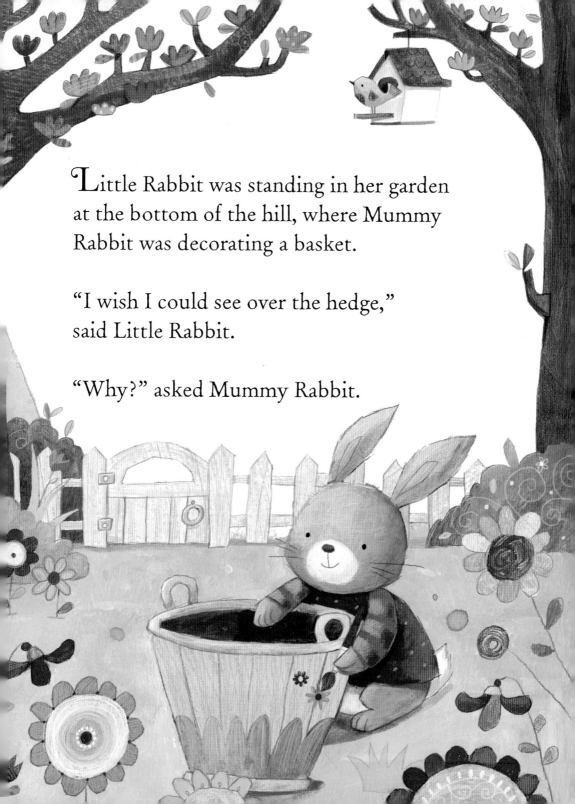

Little Rabbit was standing in her garden
at the bottom of the hill, where Mummy
Rabbit was decorating a basket.

"I wish I could see over the hedge,"
said Little Rabbit.

"Why?" asked Mummy Rabbit.

"Because I wonder what's on the other side," said Little Rabbit. "Our garden is nice, but I've never seen outside it. I'd love to know what's there."

"Shall we have a peep?" said Mummy Rabbit.

"Oh yes please," said Little Rabbit, jumping up and down. "Please can I see?"

"Of course," said Mummy Rabbit. "Just climb onto my back and hold tight." So Little Rabbit did.

Mummy Rabbit walked over to the tallest tree in the garden, and she hopped onto the lowest branch, and then the next one, and the next one...

"Look!" said Little Rabbit. "There's a lane! And it has a squirrel on it. Hello!"

"Hello," said Squirrel. "Why are you up there?"

"I thought there might be
something nice behind the
hedge," said Little Rabbit.
"And I was right. Would
you like to come and play?"

So Squirrel came round, and they all made friends
and had cakes and tea.

And that's where this story might have ended.

But then Little Rabbit looked up at the hill next
to the garden, and she started thinking again.

"Hmmm," she said, "I can't see the other side of
the hill, and I'd so love to know what's there.
But the hill is ever so tall, even taller than a hedge,
so we'll never be able to see, will we?"

And then Mummy Rabbit did a strange thing.

She walked over to the basket, which she had finished decorating, and hopped inside.

"Come on," she said. So they all got inside it. Then she tied a big piece of cloth to the top.

"Now everyone," she said, "hold on tight."

Suddenly there was a big gust of wind. Leaves were being blown off the trees and swirling around them, and the basket started to rock and bump along the ground. At first nothing else seemed to happen, but then Little Rabbit noticed something.

"We're not on the ground anymore!" she said. "The garden is getting further away."

"Yes," said Mummy Rabbit,
"we're in a ..."

"Balloon!" said Squirrel.
"It's a balloon!"

Little Rabbit held onto the basket, and stared.

First she saw the other side of the hedge, where she had met Squirrel, and then as the balloon got higher she saw the top of the hill getting closer and closer, until the basket rose right over it and climbed high into the bright blue sky.

And now, on the other side of the hill, she could see meadows and woods and streams and little lanes stretching far, far into the distance, getting smaller and smaller as the balloon got higher.

"Oh my," said Little Rabbit. "What's that?"

"That," said Mummy Rabbit, "is the world. And one day when you're big, you'll go and see it, and you'll be far away, over the hills somewhere."

Little Rabbit kept staring for a while.

"There's a lot of world, isn't there?" she said. "I don't think I want to be big just yet."

After a while they started to drift back down.

"Look!" said Little Rabbit. "I can see the garden again. And there's the tree we climbed, and the lane where Squirrel was. It all looks ever so small. Oh it will be nice to be back home. Can we have cakes and tea again?"

"Of course," said Mummy Rabbit.

And as they drifted gently back home in their balloon, they turned to wave at the enormous world as it slowly dipped out of sight behind the curve of the hill.

Badger's Happy Feeling

One winter's afternoon,
Badger was feeling a little bit sad.

"You seem very quiet today," said Badger's
friend Mouse. "Are you OK?"

Badger sighed.

"I had a really happy feeling yesterday," he said.
"But today I've lost it. I don't know where it could
have gone."

Mouse had a think.

"Well," she said, "we'd better look for it. Have you
checked in all your pockets?"

"No," said Badger, "you don't understand.
It won't be in my pocket."

"Come along," said Mouse, "let's search over
here." And she peered under the sofa. "No,"
she said, "I can't see a happy feeling under there."

So she went over to the cupboard and started
opening the drawers. She found socks and sweaters
and books and blankets, and a spider... but no
happy feeling.

"You had it yesterday," she said. "So it can't be too far away."

"Mouse," said Badger, "I think you're being silly. We can't just find a happy feeling by looking for one in the cupboards. What a silly idea."

"There's no need to be rude," said Mouse. "I'm only trying to help."

"Well, you're not helping," said Badger. "You're not helping at all."

Mouse didn't like Badger saying this, so she hurried over to the door and went out. She stared around the snowy garden to see if there might be a happy feeling hiding in a tree or under a bush, but she couldn't see one.

Then she had an idea.

She hurried down the hill and into the town,
where she stopped outside a cake shop and
peeped through the window.

She could see all kinds of exciting treats behind
the glass, so she went inside. A mole was standing
behind the counter with a welcoming smile.

"What can I get for you?" he said. "I've got tasty cakes, or sherbet lemons, or raspberry ice cream."

"That sounds lovely," said Mouse, "but I need something else. It's for my friend Badger."

"Chocolates?" said the mole. "Vanilla fudge?"

"Not exactly," said Mouse. "I'm actually looking for a happy feeling."

"Hmmm," said the mole, and he peered inside his jars of sweets. "What flavour is it?"
"I'm not sure," said Mouse.
"How about some hazelnut twirls?" said the mole.
"I don't think so," said Mouse. "Thanks anyway."

Then she went to the next shop, which was bigger and sold all sorts of different clothes.

"Hello there," said the beaver behind the counter.
"What would you like? A nice new hat?"
"Um, I need something for a friend," said Mouse.

"I've got a lovely waistcoat here," said the beaver.

"What I need is, um, a happy feeling," said Mouse.
"I don't suppose you sell any of those?"

"A happy feeling," said the beaver. "What size?"
"Oh," said Mouse, "I'm not sure."
"Is it for indoors or outdoors?" said the beaver.
"Well, sort of both I think," said Mouse.

The beaver looked puzzled. "I've got a pair
of beautiful boots," he said. "How about these?"

"No thanks," said Mouse, and she walked to the
next shop. This was the biggest shop in the whole
town and it sold all kinds of different things.

Mouse stood and gazed at the shelves inside, which
were stacked high with everything you could
possibly think of. There were amazing toys and
exciting games, and all kinds of different presents.

"This shop," said Mouse, "is bound to have what
I'm looking for."

Then a bear popped up from behind the counter. "Roller skates?" he said. "Magic tricks? Model planes? We've got it all — whatever you need."

"That's great," said Mouse. "What I need is a feeling, a happy one. It's for my friend Badger."

The bear frowned and stared up at the shelves for quite a long time, thinking carefully. "This is the first time I've ever had to say this," he said, "but I'm afraid I can't help you. We don't have a happy feeling. I'm sorry."

Mouse sighed and walked out again. She looked at the snowy roofs and the stars in the sky and she couldn't see a happy feeling anywhere. So she walked slowly back up the hill to Badger's house.

Suddenly the door flew open, and there was Badger with an enormous smile. Mouse shook her head.

"I couldn't find one," she said. "A happy feeling, I mean. There aren't any. I haven't brought one."

"That's where you're wrong," said Badger.
"What do you mean?" said Mouse. "Where is it?"

"It's here," said Badger. And he gave Mouse a hug.
"I'm sorry I was so grumpy," he said. "Come inside and tell me all about your adventures."

"Well," said Mouse, "first I went to a cake shop."

And she told Badger the whole story while they sat by the fire, and they laughed all the way through and they didn't look once for a happy feeling.

But it was there all the same.

Dog's
Umbrella

It was a grey and cloudy morning, and Cat was bored with sitting inside on her own, so she went to see her best friend, Dog.

"Hello," said Dog, "I was thinking of going for a walk. Do you want to come?"

Just then it started to rain. Cat looked up at the sky. "That would be great," she said, "but we'll have to wait for this rain to stop, won't we?"

Dog grinned. "No we won't," he said. "I've got one of these." And he held up a long blue thing.

"What is it?" said Cat. "Does it make the rain stop?"

"No," said Dog, "it's better than that – the rain carries on falling, but we don't get wet."

He lifted it over their heads and it opened out and made a little blue roof. Cat looked up into it. "I'm not getting wet," she said. "What is it?"

"It's called an umbrella," said Dog. "Isn't it great?" They set out on their walk, keeping nice and dry. After a while they saw Fox, who was very wet indeed.

"Poor Fox," said Cat. "Can he share the umbrella?" "No," said Dog, "we don't have enough room."

"But he's ever so wet," said Cat. "Please, Dog..."

"Oh alright," said Dog. So they called out to Fox, who came and huddled under the umbrella. There was a bit less room under there now.

"My tail is sticking out," whispered Dog to Cat. "Can you move over a bit?"

Then they went around a bend in the lane and they saw someone else out in the rain.

"Oh dear," said Cat. "Badger is very wet too. Can he come under the umbrella?"

"No he can't," said Dog. "There's no room. It's not our fault if Badger didn't bring an umbrella." But Cat felt sorry for Badger, so...

Dog's Umbrella

"Badger!" she called. "Come and be dry with us." Badger turned around.

"Oh, how kind!" he said. "It looks very cosy under there. Hello Fox. Nice to see you, everyone."

And Badger squeezed under the umbrella. There was quite a lot of Badger, so everyone else ended up sticking out into the rain a little bit more. They all tried to be as small as they could, but it wasn't easy.

Dog's Umbrella

"My nose is getting wet now," said Dog.
"And my nice red scarf is going all soggy."

"Yes," said Badger, "it's a strange umbrella, isn't it?
It seems to make you quite wet."

"It's a perfectly good umbrella," said Dog.
"The problem is that it's got too many–"

"Never mind," said Cat, "it's fun sharing
it with everyone else, isn't it?"

Dog looked cross and didn't say anything.
They carried on walking, with the rain hammering
down even harder.

"Who's that over there?" said Badger. "They both
look extremely wet." Everyone looked, and they
saw that it was Squirrel and Little Rabbit, splashing
through the puddles and running towards them.

"NO!" shouted Dog. "No, no, no. There's no more room. I'm sorry, but it's my umbrella."

Cat looked a little bit unhappy, but she kept quiet.

Squirrel had big round raindrops dripping off her nose and her boots were squelching as she ran, but she didn't seem to mind.

"Hello!" she said. "Nice rain, isn't it?"
Everyone else huddled closer under the umbrella.

"What do you mean?" said Cat.

"It's fun!" said Little Rabbit, running up to join them. And she splashed her feet in the puddles.

Then everyone got a surprise. Dog started to chuckle, quietly at first, then louder and louder. Suddenly he threw his umbrella onto the ground.

"Here I go!" he shouted. And he ran over
to the puddles and started splashing about.

The others looked at him for a moment,
and nobody moved.

"But I thought you loved your umbrella
and you wanted to be dry," said Cat.

"I do love it," said Dog, "and being dry is great. But these two are right, you know – being wet is good too. Come on everyone!" And he splashed and bounced and danced in the water.

All the others started to laugh, then they all ran over and joined in. And they all got very, very wet, and they didn't mind at all.

Little Lion's
Roar

One morning, Little Lion was staring out across the valley. Three days earlier, his daddy had gone to visit Crocodile on the other side of the jungle. Little Lion was looking forward to seeing him again, and he sat watching the trees to see if anyone might be coming. But no one came, so he decided to think about something else.

"I wish I could roar," said Little Lion.
"I still can't do it."
"Don't worry," said Mummy Lion,
"you'll get the hang of it."

"But Daddy will be home soon," said Little Lion. "Can't you teach me before then?"

"OK, I'll try," said Mummy Lion. "It goes like this... R-O-A-R!" Little Lion threw back his head and tried as hard as he could... "Roo! Ree! Woo!"

"Yes," said Mummy Lion, "that's quite good." "But I want to be able to roar properly," said Little Lion. And he sat back down with a frown.

Then Little Lion's friend Monkey came swinging through the trees.
"Hello Little Lion," he said. "How are you?"
"I still can't roar," said Little Lion.
"Don't worry," said Monkey. "My noise is hard too, but I learned it in the end."

"How does it go?" said Little Lion.
"OOO! OOO!" said Monkey.

"That sounds easy," said Little
Lion. "I bet I could do that…
OOO! OOO!"
"Very good," said Monkey.

"But I want to sound like a lion,
not a monkey," said Little Lion.

Then Little Lion's friend Parrot landed on a tree.
"Hello," she said. "What are you all up to?"

"My cub's learning to roar," said Mummy Lion.
"I'm not learning anything," said Little Lion.
"How did you learn your noise, Parrot?"
 "Well, I just sort of did it," said Parrot.
"I just sort of went… S-Q-U-A-W-K!"

"Squawk!" said Little Lion.
"Gosh," said Parrot, "you squawk very well for
a Lion." Then they heard another noise.

"A-ROOOO!"
"Hello Elephant," said Parrot.
"Hello," said Elephant.
"Are you having a party?"

"Sort of," said Mummy Lion.
"Little Lion is learning lots of noises."

"Well," laughed Elephant, "you won't be able to
sound like me, I'm afraid... A-ROOOO!"
Little Lion took a deep breath. "A-roooo!" he said.

"Goodness gracious!" said Elephant. "A lion that
sounds like an elephant. Well, well, well..."

"Yes," said Parrot, "and he can squawk too."
"And he can sound just like me," said Monkey.
"But I'm not a parrot or an elephant or a monkey,"
said Little Lion. "I'm a lion, and lions go... Reee!
Rooo! Oh, I give up."

"Look," said Parrot. "I think I can see someone else coming. Over there, between the trees. Perhaps it's Cheetah. You can learn another noise." Everyone waited to see who it would be.

"I don't care who it is," said Little Lion. "I can't roar, and I'm just going to sit here and feel sorry for myself."

"Why are you going to do that, little cub?" said a familiar voice. Little Lion looked up, and saw Daddy Lion standing in front of him. And then something happened that took everyone by surprise.

"ROAR! ROAR! ROAR!" said Little Lion. "Well," said Daddy Lion, "that's..." "ROAR! ROAR! ROAR! ROAR! ROAR!" said Little Lion. And he jumped up and licked Daddy Lion on the nose.

"I didn't know you'd learned to roar while I was away," said Daddy Lion.

"I didn't," said Little Lion. "I mean, I did. I mean… ROAR! ROAR! ROAR!"

"ROAR! ROAR! ROAR!" said Daddy
Lion. And all the others laughed and cheered.

"How did you learn?" asked Daddy Lion.
"I'll tell you later," said Little Lion.
"But first I'm going to do lots more roaring."

And he threw back his head and roared and roared
as loud as he could, and the sound echoed all
across the valley, to the far side of the jungle, and
up into the evening sky.

Little Bear
and the
Clock

"When's Grandma coming?" said Little Bear.

"At three o'clock," said Daddy Bear.

"When will that be?" asked Little Bear.

Daddy Bear pointed at the clock. "When the big hand gets to the top," he said. "In twenty minutes."

Little Bear sat watching the big hand, but it hardly seemed to be moving at all.

"Can you make it go faster?" he said.

Daddy Bear came and sat down next to Little Bear.

"Actually we can make the big hand go faster," he said. "There's a special magic way, but only very clever bears can do it. Shall we try?"

"Yes please," said Little Bear.

"OK," said Daddy Bear. "First we have to stand on one leg, like this."

"Why?" said Little Bear, glancing at the big hand, which still didn't seem to have moved much.

"We just do," said Daddy Bear, "or it won't work."

So Little Bear stood on one leg.

"Good," said Daddy Bear. "Now we hop around in a big circle and shout BIM BAM BOOZLE."

Little Bear wasn't sure about this, but he very much wanted the time to go faster so he tried it.

"BIM BAM BOOZLE!" they both shouted, and hopped around in a circle for a while.

"Very good," said Daddy Bear. "That means the magic can start. But we have to keep it going."

"I'm ready," said Little Bear. "What's next?"

"Next," said Daddy Bear, "you have to climb on my shoulders and then we jump up and down three times. Quickly, or the magic will stop."
So Little Bear climbed up, and they jumped.

"Very good," said Daddy Bear. "Now you have to chase me round the room, shouting out the three things that you like best."

"But I can't think of anything," said Little Bear.

"No time to lose," said Daddy Bear.

"OK," said Little Bear, "CHOCOLATE! SNOWY DAYS! MY BIG RED HAT!"

And he chased his daddy round and round the room, shouting out his favourite things.

"STOP!" said Daddy Bear. "Now close your eyes and imagine you're in a cave full of gold, and there's a dragon snoozing in the corner..."

"Yes," said Little Bear, "I'm sneaking along on my tiptoes and I'm going to get the gold. The dragon won't wake up because I'm going ever so quietly."

"That's good," said Daddy Bear, "but now it's time to open your eyes."

So Little Bear opened his eyes... and there was Grandma Bear standing at the door. Little Bear looked at the clock. The big hand was at the top.

"Hello!" said Little Bear, and he gave his granny a big hug. "Please can I show you how the magic works?" he asked.

"Of course," said Grandma Bear.

"OK," said Little Bear, "first we all stand on one leg and go around in a circle."

And they did the whole thing all the way through without stopping, and before they knew it, it was nearly time for dinner. "It really does work," said Little Bear with a chuckle.

And it does you know – give it a try sometime.

Turtle
and the
Fish

One day, Turtle was swimming deep in the sea when he met two little fish.

"Hello there," said Clown Fish. "Please could we ask you a question?"

"Of course," said Turtle.

"Our friend says that the whole world isn't water," said Angel Fish. "He says there's a place called Land, but we don't believe him. Is it true?"

"Oh yes," said Turtle, "your friend's right. If you swim up and up and up, eventually there's no more ocean and everything is different."

"No more ocean?" said Angel Fish.

"None at all," said Turtle.

"But how do the fish up there swim if there's no water?" asked Angel Fish.

"They don't swim," said Turtle, "and they aren't exactly fish. They do something called walking. It's like a sort of dance."

Clown Fish and Angel Fish started to laugh. "It all sounds very strange and silly," said Clown Fish. "Are you sure you're not making it up?"

"If you like," said Turtle, "I can show you."
The two fish stared at each other.

"You mean we could actually see it for ourselves?"
said Angel Fish. "The place where the fish aren't
really fish and they don't like water?"

"Of course," said Turtle, "as long as you
don't mind a big long swim. And we can
only see it for a moment, because you two
can't spend very long out of the water."

"OK then," said Clown Fish. "Let's do it.
Let's go there right now!"

So they all started swimming up through
the water, up and up and further up.

Eventually, after they had swum for a very long
time, the water started getting lighter above them.

"OK everyone," said Turtle, "when I count to five we'll be there, so get ready. One, two, three, four... FIVE!"

And suddenly their heads were popping
up above the water into the sunshine
and the air, and the fish
stared in amazement.

Turtle and the Fish

"What's that huge thing up there?" said Angel Fish.

"That's called the sky," said Turtle.

"And what are those?" asked Angel Fish.

"Those," said Turtle, "look like a cat and a dog."

"Hello!" called Angel Fish. "We're from the sea!"

"Oh!" shouted Cat. "Well, I'm Cat, and this is Dog. It's nice to meet you."

"Can you do some walking?" called Angel Fish.

So Cat and Dog walked along the beach. As soon as they started moving the fish wanted to laugh. But they managed not to.

"Very good!" said Angel Fish. "Thank you!"

"It's time to go, I'm afraid," said Turtle.

"Already?" said Clown Fish. "Oh no..."
"Lovely to meet you!" shouted Angel Fish.

And Cat and Dog stood and waved goodbye as the other animals dipped beneath the waves again. They all started to swim down into the water, and everyone was very excited.

"I liked the Cat Fish best," said Angel Fish.
"The Dog Fish was good too," said Clown Fish.

"And the sky was quite good too," said Angel Fish. "But it was slightly too big, I thought."

By the time they stopped talking about the world above the waves, they had swum all the way home. They never went to the surface again, but they never forgot it. And sometimes they would think about Cat and Dog with a little smile.

"Do you think maybe they think about us too?" Angel Fish would say.
"I hope sometimes they do," Clown Fish would say.

And sometimes they did.

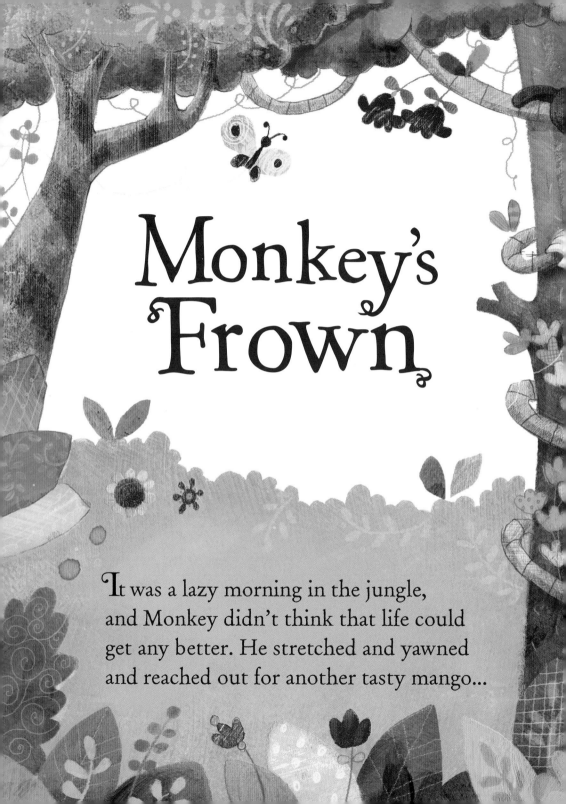

Monkey's Frown

It was a lazy morning in the jungle, and Monkey didn't think that life could get any better. He stretched and yawned and reached out for another tasty mango...

...but then a fly landed on his nose.
"Oh dear," he said, "go away…"
And as he tried to wave the fly away,
a little frown appeared on his face.

Just then, Monkey's friend Parrot landed on the tree. "Hello," she said. "Why are you frowning?"

"I'm not frowning," said Monkey.

"Yes you are," said Parrot. "You look grumpy."

"Well I'm not," said Monkey. "And I wish you'd stop saying so. Can't you leave me alone?"

Then a frown appeared on Parrot's face too, and she flew off over the treetops. After a while, she saw Little Lion playing with Elephant by the river.

"Hello," said Little Lion. "Why are you frowning?"

"Am I frowning?" said Parrot. "Oh dear."
Then a frown appeared on Little Lion's face too.

"Now you're doing it," said Parrot. "It's spreading!"

"What's that?" said Elephant, with a frown.

"Aaargh!" said Parrot. "We must stop frowning."

Then Daddy Lion came walking through the trees. "What's happening?" he said. "Are you OK?"

"There's a frown going round," said Little Lion. "We've all got it and we don't know why."

Daddy Lion thought for a moment, and a big frown slowly appeared on his face.

"OH NO!" shouted all the others.

And then, just when there was so much frown around that they almost couldn't bear it, they heard a voice.

"Hello down there!" it said. Everybody looked up, and there was Monkey sitting in a tree.

"Goodness me," he said. "What's going on?"

"You should know," said Parrot. "You started it."
"I did?" said Monkey. "When?"

"This morning," said Parrot. "You were frowning, and look what you've done now."

"Oh, I see," said Monkey. "Sorry, everyone."
"But why were you frowning?" called Daddy Lion.

"Yes," said Parrot, "what started all this?"

Everyone waited to hear what Monkey would say.
"I think," he said, "it was because a fly landed on
my nose."

For a few seconds
there was silence
and then...

"Ha ha ha ha!"

They all turned to look, and they saw Little Lion
rolling around on the floor with laughter.

"You mean we've all been frowning just because
a fly landed on your nose?" he said. "Ha ha ha!"

And then Parrot noticed something interesting. "Look," she said, "he's not frowning anymore."

"You're right," said Daddy Lion, "maybe you can't frown and laugh at the same time?"

"In that case," said Monkey, "let me help." And he sprang down and started to tickle Parrot.

"Oh!" she said, "it makes me wriggle when you tickle my feathers like that... A-HA-HA-HA!" And as she laughed, her frown vanished too.

"Can you tickle me now?" said Elephant. And as Monkey kept tickling, the laugh spread through them all, until they were shaking and squeaking and helplessly howling.

And they were laughing so hard that they hardly even noticed that there were no frowns left at all.

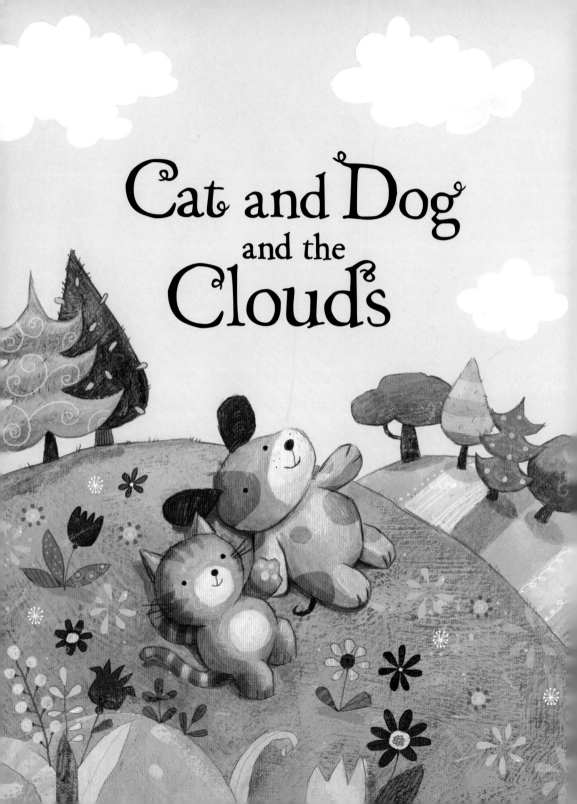

Cat and Dog
and the
Clouds

Cat and Dog were lying on the hillside,
looking up at the sky.

"Look at the clouds," said Dog.
"They have amazing shapes today.
That one looks like a dragon."

"I think it looks more like a bird,"
said Cat.

"A bird?" said Dog. "No, it's definitely a dragon. Look – there are its jaws."

"Oh yes, I see what you mean," said Cat. She looked at the cloud as it drifted across the sky.

"You don't suppose it might really be a dragon, do you?" she said. "It looks just like one."

"Of course not," said Dog. "And even if it was a dragon, I wouldn't be frightened. I'd bark so loud that it would fly away and never bother us again."

"Gosh," said Cat, "you must be brave." She looked up at the sky again. "The cloud looks different now," she said. "Now it looks like a giant strawberry."

"A strawberry?" said Dog. "No, now it looks like a wolf. You can see its long tail and its ears."

"Oh dear," said Cat, "yes, it's like a scary wolf."

"You're scared of wolves?" said Dog. "Wolves don't scare me. If that cloud was a wolf, I'd show him my teeth and he'd go running to his mother."

"I never knew you were quite so brave as that," said Cat. She peeped at the wolf to see if it was coming closer, but the cloud had changed again.

"Look," she said, "it looks like a teapot now."
"I see what you mean," said Dog, "but I think it looks more like a monster."
"A monster?" whispered Cat. "Oh dear, monsters are the scariest things of all."

"You really aren't very brave, are you?" laughed Dog. "If that cloud was a monster, I'd chase it away, like this." He leapt up and started walking towards the monster in the sky.

"Now then Mr Monster!" he shouted. "You'd better go away, or I'll have you for my supper!" "You wouldn't be scared of the monster, even a tiny bit?" said Cat.

"Not even a tiny bit," said Dog. "I'd run towards it, like this, and I'd open my jaws ever so wide and then I'd say – AAAAAAH! Help!"

"Dog," said Cat, "what's the matter?" Dog was staring down at the grass, hopping from one foot to the other.

"There's a... there's a... a spider!" he squeaked.

Cat ran over to Dog and saw a little spider in the grass. "Yes," she said, "but why did you shout?"

"Because I'm... I'm scared of spiders!" shouted Dog. "Take it away! It might crawl on my toes."

Cat and Dog and the Clouds

Cat started laughing. "But I thought you were ever so brave?" she said.

"I'm very brave!" cried Dog. "Has the sp-spider gone away now? C-Can I open my eyes?"

"Yes," said Cat, "I think it's gone now."

Dog slowly opened his eyes and peered at the grass. "Thank goodness for that," he said.

Cat was still laughing a little bit. "You won't tell anyone I'm scared of spiders, will you?" said Dog.

"No," said Cat, "of course not."

"Because I'm very big and very brave," said Dog.

"Yes," smiled Cat, "of course you are."
She looked back at the cloud.

102

"I think it looks like a butterfly now," she said.

Dog looked up at the cloud and thought for a moment. "Yes," he said, "I think it does too."

"Oh good," said Cat. "What a nice thing for the cloud to be."

And they lay on the hillside together, watching the cloud drift along. After a while it changed again and looked like something else. But they didn't see what it was, because they were fast asleep.

Digital imaging by John Russell and Nick Wakeford.

First published in 2012 by Usborne Publishing Ltd, Usborne House, 83-85 Saffron Hill, London, EC1N 8RT. Copyright © 2012 Usborne Publishing Ltd. The name Usborne and the devices 🎈 🌐 are Trade Marks of Usborne Publishing Ltd. All rights reserved. No part of this publication may be reproduced, stored in a retrieval system or transmitted in any form or by any means, electronic, mechanical, photocopying, recording, or otherwise, without the prior permission of the publisher. UKE.